PAPERBACK **PLUS**

Contents

Jane Yolen

Have you ever heard of a "sense of wonder"? Jane Yolen calls it her sixth sense. It opens the world of make-believe to her. As a child, she developed her sixth sense by reading fairy tales and playing King Arthur and Robin Hood with her brother and her best friend. Now her sixth sense helps her weave her own tales of dragons, mermaids, and giants.

● Meet the Illustrator ●

Diane Stanley

At one time, Diane Stanley's job was to draw detailed pictures of different parts of the human body for science books used by doctors. But she gave up her career as a medical illustrator when she became enchanted by the pictures in the books she read aloud to her daughters. She decided to become a children's book illustrator. She has illustrated over twenty-five children's books.

JANE YOLEN
SLEEPING UGLY

pictures by DIANE STANLEY

HOUGHTON MIFFLIN COMPANY
BOSTON
ATLANTA   DALLAS   GENEVA, ILLINOIS   PALO ALTO   PRINCETON

Acknowledgments

For each of the selections listed below, grateful acknowledgment is made for permission to excerpt and/or reprint original or copyrighted materials, as follows:

Selections

"About Sleep," by Marci Ridlon Carafoli, from *Cricket* magazine, December 1974, Vol. II, No. 4. Copyright © 1974 by Marci Ridlon. Reprinted by permission of *Cricket* magazine.

"Check Out Some of These Dreamy Facts," from *Lights Out!*, by Lisa Feder, from *3-2-1 Contact* magazine, September 1988. Copyright © 1988 by Children's Television Workshop. Reprinted by permission.

"Sleeping Beauty," by Charles Perrault, from *Sleeping Beauty and Other Stories,* retold by Margaret Carter. Copyright © 1993 by Grisewood & Dempsey Ltd. Reprinted by permission of Kingfisher Books.

Sleeping Ugly, by Jane Yolen. Text copyright © 1981 by Jane Yolen. Illustrations copyright © 1981 by Diane Stanley Vennema. Reprinted by permission of Coward, McCann & Geoghegan, Inc., a division of The Putnam & Grosset Group.

Illustrations

65–69 Andrea Barrett.   **70–71** Don Stewart.   **72** Robin Spowart.

Photography

ii Jason Stample/Jane Yolan.

Houghton Mifflin Edition, 1996

ISBN: 0-395-73227-1

123456789-B-99 98 97 96 95

Princess Miserella
was a beautiful princess
if you counted her eyes
and nose and mouth
and all the way
down to her toes.

But inside,
where it was hard to see
she was the meanest,
wickedest,
and most worthless
princess around.

She liked
stepping on dogs.
She kicked kittens.

She threw pies
in the cook's face.
And she never—
not even once—
said thank you
or please.
And besides,
she told lies.

In that very same kingdom,
in the middle of the woods,
lived a poor orphan
named Plain Jane.
She certainly was.
Her hair was short
and turned down.
Her nose was long
and turned up.
And even if they had been
the other way 'round,
she would not have been
a great beauty.
But she loved animals,
and she was always kind
to strange old ladies.

One day Princess Miserella
rode out of the palace
in a huff.
(A huff is not a kind
of carriage.
It is a kind

of temper tantrum.
Her usual kind.)
She rode and rode and rode,
looking beautiful
as always,
even with her hair in tangles.

She rode right into
the middle of the woods
and was soon lost.
She got off her horse
and slapped it sharply
for losing the way.

14

The horse said nothing,
but ran right back home.
It had known
the way back
all the time,
but it was not about
to tell Miserella.

So there was the princess,
lost in a dark wood.
It made her look
even prettier.

Suddenly,
Princess Miserella
tripped
over a little old lady
asleep under a tree.

Now little old ladies
who sleep under trees
deep in a dark wood
are almost always
fairies in disguise.
Miserella guessed

who the little old lady was,
but she did not care.
She kicked the old lady
on the bottoms of her feet.
"Get up and take me home,"
said the princess.

So the old lady
got to her feet
very slowly—
for the bottoms now hurt.
She took Miserella
by the hand.
(She used only
her thumb and second finger
to hold Miserella's hand.
Fairies know quite a bit
about *that* kind of princess.)

They walked and walked
even deeper into the wood.
There they found
a little house.
It was Plain Jane's house.

It was dreary.
The floors sank.
The walls stank.
The roof leaked
even on sunny days.

But Jane made the best of it.
She planted roses
around the door.

And little animals
and birds
made their home with her.
(That may be why
the floors sank
and the walls stank,
but no one complained.)

"This is not *my* home,"
said Miserella
with a sniff.
"Nor mine," said the fairy.
They walked in
without knocking,
and there was Jane.
"It is mine," she said.
The princess looked at Jane,
down and up,
up and down.
"Take me home," said Miserella,
"and as a reward
I will make you my maid."

Plain Jane smiled
a thin little smile.
It did not improve her looks
or the princess's mood.
"Some reward,"
said the fairy to herself.
Out loud she said,
"If you could take
both of us home,
I could probably squeeze out
a wish or two."

28

"Make it three,"
said Miserella
to the fairy,
"and *I'll* get us home."

Plain Jane smiled again.
The birds began to sing.
"My home is your home,"
said Jane.
"I like your manners,"
said the fairy.
"And for that good thought,
I'll give three wishes to *you*."

Princess Miserella
was not pleased.
She stamped her foot.
"Do that again,"
said the fairy,
taking a pine wand
from her pocket,
"and I'll turn your foot
to stone."

Just to be mean,
Miserella
stamped her foot again.
It turned to stone.

Plain Jane sighed.
"My first wish is
that you change her foot back."
The fairy made a face.
"I like your manners,
but not your taste,"
she said to Jane.
"Still, a wish is a wish."
The fairy moved the wand.
The princess shook her foot.
It was no longer made of stone.

"Guess my foot fell asleep
for a moment," said Miserella.
She really liked to lie.
"Besides," the princess said,
"that was a stupid way
to waste a wish."
The fairy was angry.
"Do not call someone stupid
unless you have been
properly introduced," she said,
"or are a member
of the family."
"*Stupid, stupid, stupid,*"
said Miserella.
She hated to be told
what to do.

"Say stupid again,"
warned the fairy,
holding up her wand,
"and I will make toads
come out of your mouth."
"Stupid!" shouted Miserella.
As she said it,
a great big toad
dropped out of her mouth.

"Cute," said Jane,
picking up the toad,
"and I *do* like toads, but . . ."
"But?" asked the fairy.
Miserella did not open her mouth.
Toads were among
her least favorite animals.
"But," said Plain Jane,
"my second wish
is that you get rid
of the mouth toads."

"She's lucky it wasn't
mouth elephants,"
mumbled the fairy.
She waved the pine wand.
Miserella opened
her mouth slowly.
Nothing came out
but her tongue.
She pointed it
at the fairy.

38

Princess Miserella
looked miserable.
That made her look
beautiful, too.
"I definitely
have had enough," she said.
"I want to go home."
She grabbed Plain Jane's arm.

"Gently, gently,"
said the old fairy,
shaking her head.
"If you are not gentle
with magic,
none of us will go anywhere."
"You can go where you want,"
said Miserella,
"but there is only one place
I want to go."
"To sleep!" said the fairy,
who was now much too mad
to remember
to be gentle.
She waved her wand
so hard
she hit the wall
of Jane's house.

The wall broke.
The wand broke.
The spell broke.
And before Jane
could make her third wish,
all three of them
were asleep.

It was one of those
famous
hundred-year-naps
that need a prince
and a kiss
to end them.
So they slept
and slept
in the cottage in the wood.
They slept through
three and a half wars,
one plague,
six new kings,
the invention of
the sewing machine,
and the discovery
of a new continent.

The cottage
was deep in the woods
so very few princes
passed by.
And none of the ones who did
even tried the door.

At the end of
one hundred years
a prince named Jojo
(who was the youngest son
of a youngest son
and so had no gold
or jewels
or property to speak of)
came into the woods.
It began to rain,

so he stepped into the cottage
over the broken wall.

He saw three women
asleep
with spiderwebs
holding them to the floor.
One of them was
a beautiful princess.

Being the kind
of young man
who read fairy tales,
Jojo knew just what to do.

But because he was
the youngest son
of a youngest son,
with no gold or jewels
or property to speak of,
he had never
kissed anyone before,
except his mother,
which didn't count,
and his father,
who had a beard.

Jojo thought he should
practice
before he tried
kissing the princess.
(He also wondered
if she would like
marrying a prince
with no property
or gold
or jewels to speak of.
Jojo knew
with princesses
that sort of thing
really matters.)
So he puckered up
his lips
and kissed the old fairy
on the nose.

It was quite pleasant.
She smelled slightly
of cinnamon.
He moved on to Jane.
He puckered up
his lips
and kissed her
on the mouth.
It was delightful.
She smelled of wild flowers.

He moved on to
the beautiful princess.
Just then the fairy
and Plain Jane
woke up.
Prince Jojo's kisses
had worked.
The fairy picked up
the pieces of her wand.
Jane looked at the prince
and remembered
the kiss
as if it were a dream.
"I wish he loved me,"
she said softly to herself.
"Good wish!" said the fairy
to herself.
She waved the two pieces
of wand gently.

The prince looked
at Miserella,
who was having a bad dream
and enjoying it.
Even frowning
she was beautiful.

But Jojo knew
that kind of princess.
He had three cousins
just like her.
Pretty on the outside.
Ugly within.

He remembered the smell
of wild flowers
and turned back to Jane.
"I love *you*," he said.
"What's your name?"

So they lived
happily ever after
in Jane's cottage.
The prince fixed the roof
and the wall
and built a house next door
for the old fairy.

They used the
sleeping princess
as a conversation piece
when friends came to visit.
Or sometimes
they stood her up
(still fast asleep)
in the hallway
and let her hold coats and hats.
But they never let anyone
kiss her awake,
not even their children,
who numbered three.

Moral:
Let sleeping princesses lie
or lying princesses sleep,
whichever seems wisest.

64

Sleeping Beauty

retold by Margaret Carter
based on the tale by Charles Perrault

In a land far away, where the sun always shines and everyone is happy, there lived a king and queen with one baby daughter.

"We must have a splendid party for her christening," said the king, and he invited all the kingdom, including the twelve good fairies who lived there. But he forgot to invite the thirteenth fairy, who was not at all good. Far from it!

On the day of the christening each fairy brought the baby a gift. One said the princess would sing like a bird, another that she would dance like a feather, and so on until it was the last fairy's turn.

Just then the thirteenth fairy, who had been hiding behind a curtain, came out. "The princess will indeed be all that my sisters have said," she said. "But on her sixteenth birthday she will prick her finger on a spindle and die!" And the wicked fairy vanished.

"The princess shall not die," said a voice, and out stepped the last fairy, who had not yet given her gift. "Instead, she will sleep for a hundred years."

At once the king forbade anyone in the kingdom to use a spinning wheel, and for sixteen years the princess was safe. But on her sixteenth birthday she found a room where she had never been before. And in it was on old woman spinning.

"What are you doing?" asked the princess. "Spinning, my dear," said the woman, who was really the wicked fairy in disguise. "Would you like to try?"

The princess stretched out her hand, and pricked her finger. "Oh!" she cried.

She yawned, rubbed her eyes, and fell into a deep sleep. All through the palace clocks did not strike, dogs stopped barking, everybody slept. And they slept for one hundred years, until a prince came wandering by and found all these people fast asleep. At last he came to the room where the princess lay. "How lovely she is!" he said, and bent to kiss her.

She stretched, she yawned, she opened her eyes. The spell was broken!

Then the clock struck, the dog gnawed his bone, and the prince and princess stood and watched everyone waking up.

"Welcome, Prince," said the king. "We'd better send out the wedding invitations!"

"Don't forget the fairies," said the queen. But that bad fairy was never seen again.

About Sleep

JOHN: I haven't slept for ten days.
BILL: Aren't you tired?
JOHN: No, I sleep nights.

SUE: I spent ten hours over my science book last night.
MARY: You did?
SUE: Yes, it fell under my bed.

Why did the little boy put hay in his bed?
To feed his nightmare.

SAM: I had a dream last night that I ate a
five-pound marshmallow.

JOE: So what?

SAM: When I woke up, my pillow was gone!

TEACHER: Tom, you can't sleep in my class!

TOM: I could if you didn't talk so loud.

Why do dragons sleep in the daytime?
Because they like to hunt knights.

Check out some of these

Dreamy Facts

- **We dream in color.**

- **Blind people have dreams too. Their dreams consist of smells, sounds and feelings — things that they sense rather than see.**

- **The dreamer usually watches the action instead of playing a part.**

- **Many of our dreams take place in familiar places: One-third of them in a house, one-quarter in trains, buses, planes or cars.**

- **Forty percent of the time, the people in our dreams are strangers.**